D0569497

PUMA RANGE

SMITHSONIAN
WILD HERITAGE COLLECTION

For Sara, Avery and Willie,
may you keep one foot in the stars
and one upon the land.

— M.A.

For my mother.

— S.G.

Illustration copyright © 1994 Simon Galkin.
Book copyright © 1994 Trudy Corporation, 353 Main Avenue,
Norwalk, CT 06851 and the Smithsonian Institution, Washington, DC 20560.

Soundprints is a Division of Trudy Corporation, Norwalk, Connecticut.

All rights reserved. No part of this book may be reproduced or
transmitted in any form or by any means whatsoever without prior
written permission of the publisher.

Book Design: Shields & Partners, Westport, CT

First Edition 1994
10 9 8 7 6 5 4 3 2
Printed in Singapore

Acknowledgements:
   Our very special thanks to Dr. Charles Handley of the department of
vertebrate zoology at the Smithsonian's National Museum of Natural History
for his curatorial review.

Library of Congress Cataloging-in-Publication Data

Armour, Michael C.

Puma range / by Michael C. Armour ;
illustrated by Simon Galkin.
                p.   cm.
Summary: When Little Puma is separated from her mother and brothers, she is
not sure that she can stay alive and find her way home alone.
        ISBN 1-56899-054-5   ISBN 1-56899-202-5 (pbk.)
1. Pumas — Juvenile fiction. [1. Pumas — Fiction. 2. Self-confidence — Fiction.]
I. Galkin, Simon, ill. II. Title.
        PZ10.3.A862Pu 1994   94-926
        (E) — dc20   CIP
                                                                           AC

PUMA RANGE

by Michael C. Armour
Illustrated by Simon Galkin

Soundprints

A Division of Trudy Corporation
Norwalk, Connecticut

On a stormy night in late spring, a puma, swollen and tired, climbed high into the western mountains. Lightning slashed across the sky. Rain filled the creekbeds and roared down the rocks. But the puma did not rest. Onward and onward she trudged. Finally, she crossed high above the canyon on a fallen birch tree, and found the cave.

That night, while thunder shook the hills, she gave birth to four spotted cubs. Little Puma, the smallest and only girl, snuggled with her brothers close to Mother's side as the storm roared outside the cave.

The next morning the cloud-line drifted west, and
the sun rose golden and warm. In the high perch of her
shallow cave, Mother Puma lay with her new cubs.
Looking out over the wide world of her range, she saw
cliffs dropping into canyons and meadows bursting
with spring. In the next few weeks, the time would come
for Mother to leave on short trips to hunt for
food for her cubs.

As the days passed, the cubs grew stronger. Soon they were playing hide and seek, stalk and pounce, scamper and tumble. Smaller and not as quick, Little Puma often kept to herself. When her brothers rushed out of the cave to play swat with her, she slinked away and hid.

One day the skies darkened again with storm. Leaving her cubs in the safety of the cave, Mother gathered food in the aspen forests nearby. It would still be several months before the cubs could hunt on their own.

Suddenly, the clouds boomed and the downpour came. A big and fearsome new puma appeared. The cubs shrieked and huddled together. This strange male had stolen into Mother's range. He would be dangerous to young cubs.

The big puma drew back his whiskers, baring his sharp teeth. The cubs clustered more tightly. Slowly, he came towards them. His mouth opened wide. Suddenly, Mother leapt from a cliff ledge and landed on his back! The two lions rolled and clawed and kicked up the ground.

The cubs raced toward the cave. The stranger limped away, defeated. Mother stared after him to be sure he did not turn back.

Not as fast as her brothers, Little Puma had been kicked aside during the scuffle. No one saw her tumble over the canyon ledge. Bouncing and sliding over loose shale, she landed far below, out of sight, but uninjured. Alone and afraid, she staggered through the wind-tossed rain into the nearby woods.

Lightning boomed and wind whipped the leaves.
Little Puma found a dead white-pine and climbed
into the hole beneath it. For a long time her eyes
and ears remained wide open to the busy sights
and sounds of this new place. Then, growing
tired, she closed her eyes and slept.

Little Puma did not wake up until late the next
day. The sun was falling behind the hills and a breeze
stirred the lush grass. She was hungrier and more
frightened than she had ever been, and needed to find
her way home. Without a sound, she slipped out of
her hole and leapt across an open field. She darted into
the high underbrush along a riverbank where she
would not be seen.

She crept through the dense foliage, moving up river. That night she climbed a tree and watched a black bear wading through water pools beneath her.

An owl, swift and silent, swooped in raking her back. Little Puma wheeled and struck out with her claws. The owl screeched and flapped out of sight.

By the second day Little Puma was even hungrier than before. But her hunting skills were poor. She chased a rabbit, but lost it deep in a thicket. She scared a mouse away as she noisily stalked it through brittle leaves. But, in the greener grass surrounding a meadow Little Puma learned to bat grasshoppers — her first successful meal. Her confidence started to grow.

The next morning, while resting
in a tree, a familiar scent in the dawn
wind awoke her. She leapt down from the
branches and moved quickly up the mountain.
Lurking nearby, a coyote watched Little Puma
climb out of sight.

Scrambling from boulder to boulder, Little Puma suddenly came to a stop. She stood rock-still and gazed out across the valleys and forests below. She had seen these valleys and forests before.

Then, Little Puma approached a small scent-mound of rocks, twigs and leaves and took a deep sniff. She knew who left this mark. Swishing her tail, she continued up the mountain.

At the summit she found the fallen
birch tree. Reaching out into the air, it
formed a natural bridge over the deep canyon
below. Slowly, timidly at first, Little Puma began
to cross. Suddenly Mother Puma appeared on
the other side. Huddling close to her were Little
Puma's three brothers.

Little Puma lifted her head, and, wagging her tail, she continued across the trunk with new-found boldness. Once she was safely across, her brothers came up to her and rubbed her playfully.

Proudly, she stood waving her tail high in the western mountain air, safe at home at last.

About the Puma

Pumas are known by many names, including cougar, catamount and mountain lion. Found in wilderness areas of western North America, pumas can grow up to 200 pounds. Cubs are born with irregular black spots and rings on their tails — marks that disappear when they are half grown. These cubs stay with their mother for up to 22 months, when they are ready to go off to hunt on their own.

Chiefly nocturnal, pumas hunt deer, hares and porcupines, as well as smaller animals, such as fish, mice and even grasshoppers. Extremely shy and secretive, these cats live a solitary existence, marking their territories (about 100 square miles in size) with scent mounds of twigs, stones and dirt to ward off other pumas. They are incredibly agile and use the cover of the land for stalking and hunting their prey. They easily dart over rocks, speed through forests and climb trees. Pumas are capable of amazing leaps, with jumps recorded from 20 to 40 feet long.

Glossary

aspen: A hardwood tree that grows in sunny areas in cooler parts of North America. The aspen's range begins in Canada and extends as far south as Virginia and the mountains in Mexico.

canyon: A deep gorge between mountain walls.

creekbed: The bottom of a small stream.

foliage: The leaves of plants and trees.

range: The region that makes up an animal's territory.

riverbank: The edge of a body of flowing fresh water.

scent mound: A pile of twigs, stones, dirt and scent that a puma leaves to mark its territory.

shale: A type of rock that breaks off into thin plates or layers.

summit: The highest point of a hill or mountain.

thicket: A thick growth of small trees and underbrush on the forest floor.

Points of Interest in this Book

pp. 4–5, 24–25, 28–29 spruce.

pp. 16–17 white pine cone, aspen leaves.

pp. 18–19 mule deer, robin.

pp. 20–21 boreal owl, black bear.

pp. 22–23 vole.